Franklin Runs Away

From an episode of the animated TV series *Franklin* produced by
Nelvana Limited, Neurones France s.a.r.l. and Neurones Luxembourg S.A.

Based on the Franklin books by Paulette Bourgeois and Brenda Clark.
TV tie-in adaptation written by Sharon Jennings and illustrated by
Sean Jeffrey, Mark Koren, Joanne Rice, and Jelena Sisic.
Based on the TV episode *Franklin Runs Away*, written by Bonnie Chung.

ISBN 0-439-23821-8

12 11 10 9 8 7 6 5 4 3 2 1   1 2 3 4 5 6/0

Printed in the U.S.A.   23

First Scholastic printing, September 2001

Franklin Runs Away

SCHOLASTIC INC.

New York   Toronto   London   Auckland   Sydney
Mexico City   New Delhi   Hong Kong   Buenos Aires

FRANKLIN could count by twos and tie his shoes. He had lots of good friends and a family who loved him very much. But one day, Franklin couldn't seem to please anybody or do anything right. He decided that no one cared about him at all.

It started at breakfast.

Harriet was cranky and fussy. Franklin tried all of his funny faces, but his sister wouldn't smile.

Then Franklin's father said, "I had to put your bicycle away for you last night. That's the third time in three days."

Franklin was told there would be no bike riding for the rest of the week.

At school, Mr. Owl read *Goldilocks and the Three Bears*.

"I wish someone would eat *my* porridge," Franklin whispered to Snail.

"Franklin, this is listening time, not talking time," said Mr. Owl.

Franklin sunk low in his chair.

During recess, Fox complained that Franklin wasn't sharing the ball.

At lunchtime, Beaver changed her mind about trading desserts with Franklin.

On the bus ride home, Bear wanted his book back even though Franklin hadn't finished reading it.

And after school, Badger forgot that she had promised to play with Franklin, and went off with Rabbit instead.

Franklin trudged home. He hoped his mother
had made an extra-good snack.

But there wasn't any snack at all.

"I'll be another minute," Franklin's mother called
from the garden.

Franklin scowled. He got out bread and butter
and jam, and made a big sandwich. When his mother
found him, she also found a big mess.

"I'll clean it up," Franklin promised.

"Oh, Franklin!" moaned his mother. "Please just
go outside."

Franklin grabbed Sam and some cookies and stomped out the door. He saw Badger and Rabbit flying a kite. He saw Bear heading to the library. He saw Fox and Beaver ride by on their bicycles.

"Nobody likes me," he muttered. "Nobody cares about me at all."

Then Franklin looked at Sam.

"I'm running away!" he declared. "I'm getting a new home and a new school and new friends!"

Franklin bundled up his cookies and marched out of the yard.

Franklin stomped across the bridge and took the path through the meadow. He and his father had gone bicycling this way just the other day.

"Hmmph!" said Franklin. His father would never get to go bike riding with him ever again.

Franklin's tummy began to rumble. He remembered the cookies in his scarf. He had made them yesterday with his mother.

"You're a very big help, Franklin," she had told him.

Well, his mother would never have his help ever again, Franklin thought.

It was late afternoon, and Franklin was tired.
He thought about Harriet having her nap. He always
played with her as soon as she woke up.

Franklin wondered if Harriet would forget all
about him.

Then he remembered how proud she was the
first time she said his name.

Franklin sat down to rest. Off in the distance, he could see the park and the soccer field, the pond and the tree house. He thought about his friends having fun, and he wondered if they would miss him.

Then he remembered that his friends had wanted him to be captain of the soccer team.

Soon it would be getting dark. Franklin wondered if his parents would bother to look for him.

Then he remembered the time he was lost. His parents had found him and held him and told him how much they loved him.

Franklin looked at the setting sun and thought about eating supper with his family. He thought about finishing his homework and getting another gold star from Mr. Owl. And he thought about the soccer game tomorrow after school.

Franklin sighed a big, deep sigh. He didn't want to find a new home and new friends. He didn't want to find a new teacher.

He wanted the family who loved him and the friends who played with him and the teacher who taught him interesting things.

Franklin ran all the way back.

When he got to his yard, he saw Harriet at the window and he could smell supper on the table. His father was at the door, calling his name.

"Here I am," Franklin answered. "I'm home!"